I0639444

George Coolidge

**Poems of Childhood**

George Coolidge

**Poems of Childhood**

ISBN/EAN: 9783744707763

Printed in Europe, USA, Canada, Australia, Japan

Cover: Foto ©Andreas Hilbeck / pixelio.de

More available books at **www.hansebooks.com**

# POEMS

OF

# CHILDHOOD.

"O! dear to memory are those hours
When every pathway led to flowers."

BOSTON:
GEORGE COOLIDGE,
13 TREMONT ROW.
1861.

Electrotyped at the
BOSTON STEREOTYPE FOUNDRY.

Darrell & Moore, Printers, Boston.

---

## CHILDHOOD.

" In my poor mind it is most sweet to muse
   Upon the days gone by; to act in thought
   Past seasons o'er, and be again a child."

BLEST hour of childhood; there, and there alone,
Dance we the revels close round Pleasure's throne;
Quaff the bright nectar from the fountain springs,
And laugh beneath the rainbow of her wings.
O! time of promise, hope, and innocence,
Of trust, and love, and happy ignorance,
When every dream is heaven, in whose fair joy
Experience yet has thrown no sad alloy;
Whose pain,when fiercest, lacks the venomed pang,
Which to maturer ill doth oft belong,
When mute, and cold, we weep departed bliss,
And Hope expires on broken happiness.

(3)

## LITTLE CHILDREN.

SPORTING through the forest wide;
Playing by the water side;
Wandering o'er the heathy fells;
Down within the woodland dells;
All among the mountains wild,
Dwelleth many a little child!
In the baron's hall of pride;
By the poor man's dull fireside:
'Mid the mighty, 'mid the mean,
Little children may be seen,
Like the flowers that spring up fair,
Bright and countless every where!
In the far isles of the main;
In the desert's lone domain;
In the savage mountain-glen,
'Mong the tribes of swarthy men;
Wheresoe'er a foot hath gone;
Wheresoe'er the sun hath shone
On a league of peopled ground,
Little children may be found!
Blessings on them! they in me
Move a kindly sympathy —
With their wishes, hopes, and fears;
With their laughter and their tears;

With their wonder so intense,
And their small experience!
Little children, not alone
On the wide earth are ye known,
'Mid its labors and its cares,
'Mid its sufferings and its snares;
Free from sorrow, free from strife,
In the world of love and life,
Where no sinful thing hath trod —
In the presence of your God,
Spotless, blameless, glorified —
Little children, ye abide!

*Mary Howitt.*

## ROSY-CHEEKED APPLES.

COME here, my bairnie,
  Come here to me;
Rosy-cheeked apples
  You shall have three.
All full of honey
  They dropped from the tree —
Like your bonny self,
  All the sweeter that they're wee.

Come here, my bairnie,
  Nor shake your fair head;
You are like my own bairn,
  Long — long dead.
Ah! for lack of nourishment
  He dropped from the tree —
Like your bonny self,
  All the sweeter he was wee!

O! old, frail folk
  Are like old fruit-trees;
They cannot stand the gnarl
  Of the cold winter breeze.
But heaven takes the fruit,
  Though earth forsake the tree;
And we mourn our fairy blossoms,
  All the sweeter that they're wee.

Come here, my bairnie,
  Come here to me;
Rosy-cheeked apples
  You shall have three.
All so full of honey
  They dropped from the tree —
Like your bonny self,
  All the sweeter they are wee.

## THE MADONNA.

" I WISH I were a picture,"
　Said a prattling little boy;
" For a picture is so beautiful,
　And its face so full of joy.
There is a pretty lady
　In the parlor of mamma,
With a ribbon blue upon her head,
　And upon her breast a star.

" And she ever smiles so sweetly,
　And her soft eyes are so blue,
That I wish when I look on her
　I might be a picture too.
She is never sad like others,
　For she smiles when people die;
And she never seems to hear it
　When the funeral goes by.

" Her blue bright eyes are beaming,
　And each seems a little dream
Of the violet reflected
　In the silence of a stream.
And she always is so happy,
　Though the saddest things occur,
That I wish I were a picture,
　In a pretty frame like her.

" I wonder if a picture
    Ever thinks thoughts of its own ?
If it smiles so very sweetly,
    When we leave it all alone.
If it knows it is a picture,
    While we are speaking thus ;
But O, it is too beautiful
    To wish to be like us."

———◆———

## THE HAPPINESS OF CHILDHOOD.

SIGHING, I see yon little troop at play,
    By sorrow yet untouched, unhurt by care,
While free and sportive they enjoy to-day,
    " Content and careless of to-morrow's fare."
O, happy age ! when Hope's unclouded ray
    Lights their green path, and prompts their sim-
                ple mirth,
Ere yet they feel the thorns that lurking lay
To wound the wretched pilgrims of the earth,
Making them rue the hour that gave them birth,
    And threw them on a world so full of pain,
Where prosperous folly treads on patient worth,
    And to deaf pride misfortune pleads in vain !
Ah ! for their future fate how many fears
Oppress my heart, and fill mine eyes with tears.
                            *Charlotte Smith.*

## CHILDREN AT PLAY.

SPORT on; sport on;
A mother's thought, shadow of heavenly love,
Dwells on you. In her home, 'mid household
 cares,
Kindle up hopes, which, deep in its soft folds,
Her inmost soul has wrapped. She musing asks,
 " What *his* high fate, that boy with eagle eye,
And well-knit limbs, and proud impetuous
 thought?
A patriot, leading men, and breathing forth
His warm soul for his country? or a bard,
With holy song refining earth's cold ear?
A son, holding the torch of love to age
As its closed eye turns dimly to the grave?
Or husband, wrapping, with protecting arms,
One who leans on him in her trusting youth?"
 " And for those girls," she asks, " what gentle
 fate
Lies cradled on the softest down of time?
A rosy lot *must* garland out their years —
Those sunny eyes, with laughing spirits wild,
Those rounded limbs are all unfit for want,
Or sterner care. Gently will they be borne
On beds of flowers, beneath an azure sky."
 O dreams, fair dreams! God's dower to wo-
 man's heart!
Your light and waving curtains still suspend
Before the future, which lies dark behind.

## A PARENTAL ODE TO MY INFANT SON.

THOU happy, happy elf!
(But stop — first let me kiss away that tear) —
        Thou tiny image of myself!
(My love, he's poking peas into his ear) —
        Thou merry, laughing sprite!
        With spirits feather light,
Untouched by sorrow, and unsoiled by sin —
(Good heavens ! the child is swallowing a pin !)

        Thou little tricksy Puck !
With antic toys so funnily bestuck ;
Light as the singing bird that wings the air !
(The door ! the door ! he'll tumble down the
        stair !)
        Thou darling of thy sire !
(Why, Jane, he'll set his pinafore afire !)
        Thou imp of mirth and joy !
In love's dear chain so strong and bright a link !
Thou idol of thy parents — (Stop the boy !
        There goes my ink !)

        Thou cherub — but of earth !
Fit playfellow for fays by moonlight pale,
        In harmless sport and mirth.
(The dog will bite him if he pulls his tail !)

Thou human humming-bee, extracting honey
From every blossom in the world that blows,
   Singing in youth's Elysium ever sunny,
(Another tumble — that's his precious nose!)
     Thy father's pride and hope!
(He'll break the mirror with that skipping-rope!)
With pure heart newly stamped from Nature's
     mint,
    (Where *did* he learn that squint?)


     Thou young domestic love!
(He'll have that jug off with another shove!)
    Dear nursling of the hymeneal nest!
    (Are those torn clothes his best?)
    Little epitome of man!
(He'll climb upon the table, — that's his plan!)
Touched with the beauteous tints of dawning life,
     (He's got a knife!)
    Thou enviable being!
No storms, no clouds, in thy blue sky foreseeing;
    Play on, play on,
    My elfin John!
Toss the light ball — bestride the stick;
(I knew so many cakes would make him sick!)
With fancies buoyant as the thistle down,
Prompting the face grotesque, and antic brisk,
    With many a lamb-like frisk!
(He's got the scissors, snipping at your gown!)

Thou pretty opening rose !
(Go to your mother, child, and wipe your nose !)
Balmy, and breathing music like the south,
(He really brings my heart into my mouth !)
Fresh as the morn, and brilliant as its star,
(I wish that window had an iron bar !)
Bold as the hawk, yet gentle as the dove —
(I'll tell you what, my love,
I cannot write unless he's sent above !)

Hood.

## HOW LIKE HIS FATHER !

BEHOLD, my lords, although the print be little,
     the whole matter
And copy of the father : eye, nose, lip,
The trick of his frown, his forehead ; nay, the
     valley,
The pretty dimples of his chin, and cheek, his
     . smiles ;
The very mould of hand, nail, finger.

Shakspeare.

## MOUNTAIN CHILDREN.

DWELLERS by lake and hill,
Merry companions of the bird and bee,
  Go gladly forth and drink of joy your fill,
With unconstrainéd step and spirit free.

  No crowd impedes your way ;
No city wall proscribes your further bounds ;
  Where the wild flocks can wander, ye may stray
The long day through, mid summer sights and
    sounds.

  The sunshine and the flowers,
And the old trees that cast a solemn shade ,
  The pleasant evening, the fresh, dewy hours,
Aud the green hills whereon your fathers played :

  The gray and ancient peaks,
Round which the silent clouds hang day and
    night ;
  And the low voice of water, as it makes,
Like a glad creature, murmurings of delight ;

  These are your joys.  Go forth,
Give your hearts up unto their mighty power ;
  For in his spirit God has clothed the earth,
And speaks in love from every tree and flower.

The voice of hidden rills
Its quiet way into your spirit finds;
  And awfully the everlasting hills
Address you in their many-tonéd winds.

  Ye sit upon the earth
Twining its flowers, and shouting, full of glee;
  And a pure, mighty influence, 'mid your mirth,
Moulds your unconscious spirit silently.

  Hence is it that the lands
Of storm and mountain have the noblest sons;
  Whom the world reverences, the patriot bands
Were of the hills like you, ye little ones!

  Children of pleasant song
Are taught within the mountain solitudes;
  For hoary legends to your wilds belong,
And yours are haunts where inspiration broods.

  Then go forth: earth and sky
To you are tributary; joys are spread
  Profusely, like the summer flowers that lie
In the green path, beneath your gamesome tread.

*Mary Howitt.*

## TO J. H.

FOUR YEARS OLD—A NURSERY SONG.

> .  .  .  . Pien d' amori,
> Pien di canti, e pien di fiori.
>
> *Frugoni.*
>
> Full of little loves of ours,
> Full of songs, and full of flowers.

AH, little ranting Johnny!
Forever blithe and bonny,
And singing nonny, nonny;
With hat just thrown upon ye,
Or whistling like the thrushes,
With voice in silver gushes;
Or twisting random posies
With daisies, weeds, and roses;
And strutting in and out so,
Or dancing all about so;
With cock-up nose so lightsome,
And sidelong eyes so brightsome,
And cheeks as ripe as apples,
And head as rough as Dapple's,
And arms as sunny shining
As if their veins they'd wine in,
And mouth that smiles so truly
Heaven seems to have made it newly —

It breaks into such sweetness
With merry-lipped completeness ;
Ah, Jack, ah, Gianni mio,
As blithe as Laughing Trio !
Sir Richard, too, you rattler,
So christened from the Tatler,
My Bacchus in his glory,
My little Cor-di-fiori,
My tricksome Puck, my Robin,
Who in and out come bobbing,
As full of feints and frolics as
That fibbing rogue Antolycus,
And play the graceless robber on
Your grave-eyed brother Oberon, —
Ah, Dick, ah, Dolce-riso,
How can you, can you be so ?

One cannot turn a minute,
But mischief — there you're in it :
A-getting at my books, John,
With mighty bustling looks, John ;
Or poking at the roses,
In midst of which your nose is ;
Or climbing on a table,
No matter how unstable,
And turning up your quaint eye
And half-shut teeth, with, " Mayn't I ? "
Or else you're off at play, John,
Just as you'd be all day, John,

With hat or not, as happens ;
And there you dance, and clap hands,
Or on the grass go rolling,
Or plucking flowers, or bowling,
And getting me expenses
With losing balls o'er fences ;
Or, as the constant trade is,
Are fondled by the ladies
With, " What a young rogue this is ! "
Reforming him with kisses ;
Till suddenly you cry out,
As if you had an eye out,
So desperately tearful,
The sound is really fearful ;
When, lo ! directly after,
It bubbles into laughter.

Ah, rogue ! and do you know, John,
Why 'tis we love you so, John ?
And how it is they let ye
Do what you like and pet ye,
Though who look upon ye,
Exclaim, " Ah, John, Johnny ! "
It is because you please 'em
Still more Johnny, than you tease 'em ;
Because, too, when not present,
The thought of you is pleasant ;
Because, though such an elf, John,
They think that if yourself, John,

2

Had something to condemn too,
You'd be as kind to them too ;
In short, because you're very
Good-tempered, Jack, and merry,
And are as quick at giving
As easy at receiving,
And in the midst of pleasure
Are certain to find leisure
To think, my boy, of ours,
And bring us lumps of flowers.

But see, the sun shines brightly ;
Come, put your hat on rightly,
And we'll among the bushes,
And hear your friends, the thrushes ;
And see what flowers the weather
Has rendered fit to gather ;
And, when we home must jog, you
Shall ride my back, you rogue you, —
Your hat adorned with fine leaves,
Horse-chestnut, oak, and vine-leaves ;
And so, with green o'erhead, John,
Shall whistle home to bed, John.

*Leigh Hunt.*

## UNDER MY WINDOW.

UNDER my window, under my window,
    All in the midsummer weather,
Three little girls, with fluttering curls,
    Flit to and fro together : —
There's Bell with her bonnet of satin sheen,
And Maud with her mantle of silver green,
    And Kate with her scarlet feather.

Under my window, under my window,
    Leaning stealthily over,
Merry and clear, the voice I hear
    Of each glad-hearted rover.
Ah! sly little Kate, she steals my roses ;
And Maud and Bell twine wreaths and posies,
    As merry as bees in clover.

Under my window, under my window,
    In the blue midsummer weather,
Stealing slow, on a hushed tiptoe,
    I catch them all together : —
Bell with her bonnet of satin sheen,
And Maud with her mantle of silver green,
    And Kate with the scarlet feather.

Under my window, under my window,
　And off through the orchard closes,
While Maud she flouts, and Bell she pouts,
　They scamper and drop their posies ;
But dear little Kate takes nought amiss,
And leaps in my arms with a loving kiss,
　And I give her all my roses.

*T. Westwood.*

---

## THE GAMBOLS OF CHILDREN.

Down the dimpled greensward dancing,
　Bursts a flaxen-headed bevy —
Bud-lipped boys and girls advancing,
　Love's irregular little levy.

Rows of liquid eyes in laughter,
　How they glimmer, how they quiver !
Sparkling one another after,
　Like bright ripples on a river.

Tipsy band of rubious faces,
　Flushed with Joy's ethereal spirit,
Make your mocks and sly grimaces
　At Love's self, and do not fear it.

*George Darley.*

## A FANCY ABOUT A BOY.

" Nothing, — less than nothing ; and vanity."

WE stood beside the window, still —
  The little boy and I ;
Within the room was sober gloom ;
  Without, a sunset sky.
I drew him forward to the light,
  That I might view him plain :
The sudden view thrilled my heart through
  With a delicious pain.

I leant his head back o'er my arm,
  And smoothed his crispéd hair —
The dear, dear curls, o'er which salt pearls
  I could have rained out there.
I looked beneath his heavy lids,
  Drooping with dreamy fold :
What visioned eyes I saw arise !
  But nothing shall be told.

Gayly I spoke : " Could I count back
  Nine years, and he gain nine,
I would not say what ill to-day
  Had chanced this heart of mine."
He laughed — all laughed — I most of all ;
  But I was glad, I ween,
That the whole room lay in such gloom
  His face alone was seen.

He talked to me in schoolboy phrase;
  I gave him meet replies,
I mind not what; my sense was nought,
  Or lived but in mine eyes.
I could not kiss him as a child;
  I only touched his hair;
Or with my hand his broad brow spanned,
  But not that it was fair.

He, strange to me, as I to him —
  We never met before;
Yet I would fain brave mickle pain
  To see the lad once more.
But why this was, and is, God knows;
  And I — I know, with joy,
I'll find, among his angel-throng,
  An angel like that boy.

*Anonymous.*

## LITTLE ELLIE.

DARLING little Ellie,
  Stout of heart and limb —
What, I often wonder,
  Will the future make of him?

Where will be the roses
  That make his cheeks so red,
When years, with their temptations,
  And trials shall have fled?

Stirring with the morning,
  As if he owned the farm;
On the floor at sunset,
  Sleeping on his arm.

Torn and faded jacket,
  Feet brown and bare,
Sunshine laughing in his eyes,
  And tangled in his hair.

In his little bucket
  Helping milk the cows —
Riding on the horses,
  Tumbling down the mows;

Wading in the water,
  Working mimic mills —
Chasing through the meadows,
  Rolling down the hills;

Making strings of elm-bark,
  Stealing mother's yarn —
All to see his kite fly
  Higher than the barn;

Planning, long aforetime,
  With ambitious pride,
How, when snow has fallen,
  He'll have a sled and ride.

Gravely puzzling over
  Each childish little plan —
Working, and tugging,
  And scheming like a man.

Now upon grandfather's knee,
  Listening with delight
To the stories that are new
  Every day and night.

Now, with joyous make-believe,
  In despite his frown,
Turning chairs to railcars,
  And riding into town.

Ah, 'tis wisely well for us
  That we cannot see
What, in years that are to come,
  He will grow to be.

                              *Alice Cary.*

## TO H. C.

### SIX YEARS OLD.

O THOU, whose fancies from afar are brought;
  Who of thy words dost make a mock apparel,
And fittest to unutterable thought
  The breeze-like motion and the self-born carol;
Thou fairy voyager, that dost float
In such clear water that thy boat
May rather seem
To brood on air than on an earthly stream —
Suspended in a stream as clear as sky,
Where earth and heaven do make one imagery;
O, blessed vision! happy child!
Thou art so exquisitely wild,
I think of thee with many fears
For what may be thy lot in future years.

I thought of times when Pain might be thy guest,
  Lord of thy house and hospitality;
And Grief, uneasy lover, never rest
  But when she sat within the touch of thee.
O, too industrious folly!
O, vain and causeless melancholy!
Nature will either end thee quite;
Or, lengthening out thy season of delight,

Preserve for thee, by individual right,
A young lamb's heart among the full-grown flocks.
  What hast thou to do with sorrow,
  Or the injuries of to-morrow?
Thou art a dew-drop, which the morn brings forth,
Ill fitted to sustain unkindly shocks,
Or to be trailed along the soiling earth;
  A gem that glitters while it lives,
  And no forewarning gives,
But, at the touch of wrongs, without a strife
Slips in a moment out of life.

*William Wordsworth.*

————————

## TO GEORGE M——.

YES, I do love thee well, my child,
  Albeit mine's a wandering mind;
But never, darling, hast thou smiled,
  Or breathed a wish, that did not find
  A ready echo in my heart.
What hours I've held thee on my knee,
  Thy little rosy lips apart!
Or, when asleep, I've gazed on thee,
And with old tunes sung thee to rest,
  Hugging thee closely to my bosom;
For thee my very heart hath blessed,
  My joy, my care, my blue-eyed blossom!

*Thomas Miller.*

## TO A SLEEPING CHILD.

ART thou a thing of mortal birth,
Whose happy home is on our earth?
Does human blood with life imbue
Those wandering veins of heavenly blue,
That stray along that forehead fair,
Lost 'mid a gleam of golden hair?
O, can that light and airy breath
Steal from a being doomed to death?
Those features to the grave be sent
In sleep thus mutely eloquent?
Or, art thou, what thy form would seem,
A phantom of a blessed dream?

　A human shape I feel thou art;
I feel it at my beating heart,
Those tremors both of soul and sense
Awoke by infant innocence!
Though dear the forms by Fancy wove,
We love them with a transient love;
Thoughts from the living world intrude
Even on her deepest solitude:
But, lovely child, thy magic stole
At once into my inmost soul,
With feelings as thy beauty fair,
And left no other vision there.

　To me thy parents are unknown;
Glad would they be their child to own!

And well they must have loved befw,
If since thy birth they loved not more.
Thou art a branch of noble stem,
And, seeing thee, I figure them.
What many a childless one would give,
If thou in their still home wouldst live,
Though in thy face no family line
Might sweetly say, " This babe is mine ! "
In time thou wouldst become the same
As their own child, all but the name.
  How happy must thy parents be
Who daily live in sight of thee !
Whose hearts no greater pleasure seek
Than see thee smile, and hear thee speak,
And feel all natural griefs beguiled
By thee, their fond, their duteous child '
What joy must in their souls have stirred
When thy first broken words were heard —
Words, that, inspired by heaven, expressed
The transports dancing in thy breast !
And for thy smile ! — thy lip, cheek, brow,
Even while I gaze, are kindling now.
  I called thee duteous ; am I wrong ?
No ! truth, I feel, is in my song.
Duteous, thy heart's still beatings move
To God, to Nature, and to love !
To God ! — for thou, a harmless child,
Hast kept his temple undefiled :
To Nature ! — for thy tears and sighs

Obey alone her mysteries ;
To Love ! — for fiends of hate might see
Thou dwell'st in love, and love in thee.
What wonder then, though in thy dreams
Thy face with mystic meaning beams !
  O, that my spirit's eye could see
Whence burst those gleams of ecstasy !
That light of dreaming soul appears
To play from thoughts above thy years ;
Thou smilest as if thy soul were soaring
To heaven, and heaven's God adoring.
And who can tell what visions high
May bless an infant's sleeping eye ?
What brighter throne can brightness find
To reign on than an infant's mind,
Ere sin destroy, or error dim,
The glory of the seraphim ?
  But now thy changing smiles express
Intelligible happiness.
I feel my soul thy soul partake ;
What grief if thou wouldst now awake !
With infants happy as thyself
I see thee bound, a playful elf ;
I see thou art a darling child
Among thy playmates bold and wild ;
They love thee well ; thou art the queen
Of all their sports, in bower or green ;
And if thou livest to woman's height,
In thee will friendship, love, delight.

And live thou surely must ; thy life
Is far too spiritual for the strife
Of mortal pain ; nor could disease
Find heart to prey on smiles like these.
O, thou wilt be an angel bright—
To those thou lovest, a saving light —
The staff of age, the help sublime
Of erring youth, and stubborn prime ;
And when thou goest to heaven again,
Thy vanishing be like the strain
Of airy harp — so soft the tone
The ear scarce knows when it is gone !

## TO A CHILD.

DEAR child! whom sleep can hardly tame,
As live and beautiful as flame,
Thou glancest round my graver hours
As if thy crown of wild-wood flowers
Were not by mortal forehead worn,
But on the summer breeze were borne,
Or on a mountain streamlet's waves
Came glistening down from dreamy caves.

With bright, round cheek, amid whose glow
Delight and wonder come and go,
And eyes whose inward meanings play
Congenial with the light of day,
And brow so calm, a home for Thought
Before he knows his dwelling wrought;
Though wise indeed thou seemest not,
Thou brightenest well the wise man's lot.

That shout proclaims the undoubting mind;
That laughter leaves no ache behind;
And in thy look and dance of glee,
Unforced, unthought of, simply free,
How weak the schoolman's formal art
Thy soul and body's bliss to part!
I hail thee Childhood's very lord,
In gaze and glance, in voice and word.

In spite of all foreboding fear,
A thing thou art of present cheer ;
And thus to be beloved and known,
As is a rushy fountain's tone,
As is the forest's leafy shade,
Or blackbird's hidden serenade.
Thou art a flash that lights the whole —
A gush from nature's vernal soul.

And yet, dear child ! within thee lives
A power that deeper feeling gives ;
That makes thee more than light or air,
Than all things sweet and all things fair.
And sweet and fair as aught may be,
Diviner life belongs to thee ;
For, 'mid thine aimless joys, began
The perfect heart and will of man.

Thus, what thou art foreshows to me
How greater far thou soon shalt be ;
And while amid thy garlands blow
The winds that warbling come and go,
Ever within, not loud but clear,
Prophetic murmur fills the ear,
And says that every human birth
Anew discloses God to earth.

*John Sterling.*

CHILDHOOD.

## LITTLE CORA.

Cora's hand is dimpled —
   Very small and fair,
And its softness soothes me
   Pressing on my hair;
Cora's voice is music,
   Gushing through the hours,
Rippling in the twilight,
   " Whom we love are ours."

Cora has two natures;
   A mischief-loving sprite,
Peeping from meek eyelids
   Through fringes dark as night —
A spirit sweet and saintly
   Sitting in her smile,
With one wing in the fountain
   That sent up tears erewhile.

And here we sit together;
   Each heart with its sphinx,
Now winding — now unloosing
   Life's Gordian knotted links;
Till a mild voice whispers —
   " Ye linger, daughters, late,
And Beauty's handmaids only
   *On early sleepers wait.*"

3

God bless my Cora's mother
 For her heart of ruth,
And keep forever gleaming
 The dew-drops of her youth.
God love the rare old mansion,
 With its something dearer still
Than the white-browed children
 And the star-song's thrill !

----◆----

## MATERNAL DAYS.

To aid thy mind's development — to watch
 Thy dawn of little joys — to sit and see
Almost thy very growth — to view thee catch
 Knowledge of objects — wonders yet to thee ;
To hold thee lightly on a gentle knee,
 And print on thy soft cheek a parent's kiss ;
This, it should seem, was not reserved for me !
 Yet this was in my nature ; — as it is,
I know not what there is there, yet
 Something like to this.

          *Byron.*

## THE BAREFOOT BOY.

BLESSINGS on the little man!
Barefoot boy, with cheek of tan!
With thy turned-up pantaloons,
And thy merry whistled tunes;
With thy red lip redder still,
Kissed by strawberries on the hill;
With the sunshine on thy face
Through thy torn brim's janty grace;
From my heart I give thee joy!
I was once a barefoot boy.
Prince thou art, — the grown-up man
Only is republican.
Let the million-dollared ride, —
Barefoot, trudging at his side,
Thou hast more than he can buy,
In the reach of ear and eye:
Outward sunshine, inward joy —
Blessings on the barefoot boy!

O, for boyhood's painless play!
Sleep that wakes in laughing day,
Health that mocks the doctor's rules,
Knowledge never learned of schools;
Of the wild bee's morning chase,
Of the wild flowers' time and place,

Flight of fowl, and habitude
Of the tenants of the wood;
How the tortoise bears his shell,
How the woodchuck digs his cell,
And the ground-mole sinks his well;
How the robin feeds her young,
How the oriole's nest is hung;
Where the whitest lilies blow,
Where the freshest berries grow,
Where the ground-nut trails its vine,
Where the wood-grape's clusters shine;
Of the black wasp's cunning way,
Mason of his walls of clay;
And the architectural plans
Of gray hornet artisans:
For, eschewing books and tasks,
Nature answers all he asks;
Hand in hand with her he walks,
Face to face with her he talks,
Part and parcel of her joy —
Blessings on the barefoot boy!


O, for boyhood's time of June!
Crowding years in one brief moon;
When all things I heard or saw,
Me, their master, waited for.
I was rich in flowers and trees,
Humming-birds and honey-bees;

For my sport the squirrel played,
Plied the snouted mole his spade ;
For my taste the blackberry cone
Purpled over hedge and stone ;
Laughed the brook for my delight
Through the day and through the night, —
Whispering at the garden wall,
Talked with me from fall to fall ;
Mine the sand-rimmed pickerel pond,
Mine the walnut slopes beyond ;
Mine, on bending orchard trees,
Apples of Hesperides.
Still, as my horizon grew,
Larger grew my riches too ;
All the world I saw or knew
Seemed a complex Chinese toy
Fashioned for a barefoot boy.


O, for festal dainties spread
Like my bowl of milk and bread,
Pewter spoon and bowl of wood,
On the door-stone gray and rude !
O'er me, like a regal tent,
Cloudy-ribbed, the sunset bent ;
Purple-curtained fringed with gold,
Looped in many a wide-swung fold ;
While, for music, came the play
Of the pied frog's orchestra ;

And, to light the noisy choir,
Lit the fly his lamp of fire.
I was monarch — pomp and joy
Waited on the barefoot boy.

Cheerily, then, my little man,
Live and laugh as boyhood can ;
Though the flinty slopes be hard,
Stubble-speared the new-mown sward,
Every morn shall lead thee through
Fresh baptisms of the dew ;
Every evening, from thy feet
Shall the cool wind kiss the heat.
All too soon these feet must hide
In the prison-cells of pride ;
Lose the freedom of the sod,
Like a colt's, for work be shod ;
Made to tread the mills of toil,
Up and down in ceaseless moil :
Happy if their track be found
Never on forbidden ground ;
Happy if they sink not in
Quick and treacherous sands of sin.
Ah, that thou couldst know thy joy,
Ere it passes, barefoot boy.

*John G. Whittier.*

## THE SHADOW CHILD.

WHENCE came this little phantom,
  That flits about my room, —
That's here from early morning
  Until the twilight gloom?
Forever dancing, dancing,
  She haunts the wall and floor,
And frolics in the sunshine
  Around the open door.

The ceiling by the table
  She makes her choice retreat,
For there a little human girl
  Is wont to have her seat.
They take a dance together —
  A crazy little jig;
And sure two baby witches
  Ne'er ran so wild a rig.

They pat their hands together,
  With frantic jumps and springs,
Until you almost fancy
  You can catch the gleam of wings.
Shrill shrieks the human baby
  In the madness of delight,
And back return loud echoes
  From the little shadow sprite.

Her blue eyes are beaming,
  And each seems a little dream
Of the violet reflected
  In the silence of a stream ;
And she always is so happy,
  Though the saddest things occur,
That I wish I were a picture,
  In a pretty frame like her.

At night I still am haunted
  By glimpses of her face ;
Her features on my pillow
  By moonlight I can trace.
Whence came this shadow-baby,
  That haunts my heart and home ?
What kindly hand hath sent her,
  And wherefore hath she come ?

Long be her dancing image
  Our guest by night and day,
For lonely were our dwelling
  If she were now away.
Far happier hath our home been,
  More blest than ere before,
Since first that little shadow
  Came gliding through our door.

## LITTLE RED RIDING HOOD.

COME back, come back together,
   All ye fancies of the past :
Ye days of April weather,
   Ye shadows that are cast
     By the haunted hours before !
Come back, come back, my childhood ;
   Thou art summoned by a spell
From the green leaves of the wildwood,
   From beside the charméd well,
     For Red Riding Hood, the darling,
      The flower of fairy lore !

The fields were covered over
   With colors as she went ;
Daisy, buttercup, and clover
   Below her footsteps bent ;
     Summer shed its shining store ;
She was happy as she pressed them
   Beneath her little feet ;
She plucked them and caressed them ;
   They were so very sweet,
     They had never seemed so sweet before,
To Red Riding Hood, the darling,
     The flower of fairy lore.

How the heart of childhood dances
  Upon a sunny day!
It has its own romances,
  And a wide, wide world have they!
    A world where Phantasie is king,
Made all of eager dreaming;
  When once grown up and tall —
Now is the time for scheming —
  Then we shall do them all!
    Do such pleasant fancies spring
For Red Riding Hood, the darling,
  The flower of fairy lore?

She seems like an ideal love,
  The poetry of childhood shown,
And yet loved with a real love,
  As if she were our own —
    A younger sister for the heart;
Like the woodland peasant
  Her hair is brown and bright;
And her smile is pleasant,
  With its rosy light.
    Never can the memory part
With Red Riding Hood, the darling,
  The flower of fairy lore.

Did the painter, dreaming
  In a morning hour,
Catch the fairy seeming
  Of this fairy flower?

Winning it with eager eyes
From the old enchanted stories,
Lingering with a long delight
On the unforgotten glories
Of the infant sight?
Giving us a sweet surprise
In Red Riding Hood, the darling,
The flower of fairy lore?

Too long in the meadow staying,
Where the cowslip bends,
With the buttercups delaying
As with early friends,
Did the little maiden stay.
Sorrowful the tale for us;
We, too, loiter 'mid life's flowers,
A little while so glorious,
So soon lost in darker hours.
All love lingering on their way,
Like Red Riding Hood, the darling,
The flower of fairy lore.

*Lætitia Elizabeth Maclean.*

## WATCH, MOTHER, WATCH.

MOTHER, watch the little feet
  Climbing o'er the garden wall,
Bounding through the busy street,
  Ranging cellar, shed, and hall.
Never count the moments lost,
Never mind the time it cost ;
Little feet will go astray,
Guide them, mother, while you may.

Mother, watch the little hand
  Picking berries by the way,
Making houses in the sand,
  Tossing up the fragrant hay.
Never dare the question ask —
" Why to me this weary task ? "
These same little hands may prove
Messengers of light and love.

Mother, watch the little tongue
  Prattling eloquent and wild,
What is said, and what is sung
  By the happy, joyous child.
Catch the word while yet unspoken,
Stop the vow before 'tis broken ;
This same tongue may yet proclaim
Blessings in a Saviour's name.

Mother, watch the little heart,
　　Beating soft and warm for you ;
Wholesome lessons now impart,
　　Keep, O keep that young heart true ;
Extricating every weed ;
Sowing good and precious seed ;
Harvest rich you then may see,
Ripening for eternity.

----

## A CHILD PRAYING.

FOLD thy little hands in prayer,
　　Bow down at thy mother's knee ;
Now thy sunny face is fair,
Shining through thine auburn hair ;
　　Thine eyes are passion free ;
And pleasant thoughts, like garlands, bind thee
Unto thy home, yet grief may find thee—
　　　　Then pray, child, pray !

Now, thy young heart, like a bird,
　　Warbles in its summer nest ;
No evil thought, no unkind word,
No chilling autumn winds have stirred
　　The beauty of thy rest ;

But winter hastens, and decay
Shall waste thy verdant home away —
      Then pray, child, pray!

Thy bosom is a house of glee,
  With gladness harping at the door;
While ever, with a joyous shout,
Hope, the May queen, dances out,
  Her lips with music running o'er;
But Time those strings of joy will sever,
And Hope will not dance on forever —
      Then pray, child, pray!

Now, thy mother's arm is spread
  Beneath thy pillow in the night;
And loving feet creep round thy bed,
And o'er thy quiet face is shed
  The taper's darkened light;
But that fond arm will pass away,
By thee no more those feet will stay —
      Then pray, child, pray!

*Robert Aris Willmott.*

## LITTLE BOY BLUE.

WHEN the cornfields and meadows
    Are pearled with the dew,
With the first sunny shadow
    Walks little Boy Blue.

O, the nymphs and the graces
    Still gleam on his eyes,
And the kind fairy faces
    Look down from the skies !

And a secret revealing
    Of life within life,
When feeling meets feeling
    In musical strife.

A winding and weaving
    In flowers and in trees,
A floating and heaving
    In sunlight and breeze.

A striving and soaring,
    A gladness and grace,
Make him kneel half adoring
    The God in the place.

Then amid the live shadows
  Of lambs at their play,
Where the kine scent the meadows
  With breath like the May ; —

He stands in the splendor
  That waits on the morn,
And a music more tender
  Distils from his horn.

And he weeps, he rejoices,
  He prays ; nor in vain,
For soft loving voices
  Will answer again ;

And the nymphs and the graces
  Still gleam through the dew,
And kind fairy faces
  Watch little Boy Blue.

*Anonymous.*

## A LITTLE GIRL THAT MEETS ME.

THERE'S a little girl that meets me,
And with laughter ever greets me,
And to kiss her oft entreats me,
    As I stray
'Long the path of life, so dreary,
Where the saddened heart and weary
Shades the sunlight, shining near me,
    On my way.

She has eyes as blue as heaven —
Only aged about eleven;
But unto her God has given
    Such a heart,
That forever she is singing,
And her sweet voice, ever ringing,
Beauty o'er the rapt heart bringing,
    Sweet as art.

With her sunny hair so curly,
With her teeth so white and pearly,
I have met her, late and early,
    By the way;
And I take her hand, and press it
In my own, just to caress it —
" Pretty little hand — God bless it ! "
    I do say.

4

May the world smile kindly on her,
Benedictions fall upon her,
Angels be her guard of honor,
  As she goes
Through this world of ours, singing,
Peace to troubled spirits bringing,
No grief her poor heart wringing
  With its woes.

May the sweetest harp in heaven,
Brightest crown that e'er was given
Where the waves of life are driven
  Past the throne,
Echo to her dainty finger,
'Pon her pure brow ever linger,
While each angel is a singer,
  Calling home.

## CHILDHOOD.

CHILDHOOD! happiest stage of life!
Free from care, and free from strife,
Free from memory's ruthless reign,
Fraught with scenes of former pain;
Free from fancy's cruel skill,
Fabricating future ill;
Time when all that meets the view,
All can charm, for all is new;
How thy long-lost hours I mourn,
Never, never to return!

Then to toss the circling ball,
Caught rebounding from the wall;
Then the mimic ship to guide
Down the kennel's dirty tide;
Then the hoop's revolving pace
Through the dirty street to chase;
O what joy! it once was mine;
Childhood! matchless boon of thine!
How thy long-lost hours I mourn,
Never, never to return!

*Scott.*

## A CHILD'S SMILE.

" For I say unto you, that in heaven their angels do always
behold the face of my Father which is in heaven."

A CHILD'S smile — nothing more ;
Quiet, and soft, and grave, and seldom seen ;
    Like summer lightning o'er,
Leaving the little face again serene.

I think, boy well beloved,
Thine angel, who did grieve to see how far
    Thy childhood is removed
From sports that dear to other children are ; —

On this pale cheek has thrown
The brightness of his countenance, and made
    A beauty like his own —
That while we see it, we are half afraid,

And marvel, will it stay ?
Or, long ere manhood, will that angel fair,
    Departing some sad day,
Steal the child-smile and leave the shadow care ?

Nay, fear not.   As is given
Unto this child the father watching o'er,
His angel up in heaven
Beholds our Father's face forevermore.

And He will help him bear
His burden, as his father helps him now ;
So may he come to wear
That happy child-smile on an old man's brow.

*Miss Muloch.*

------

## CHILDHOOD.

In my poor mind it is most sweet to muse
Upon the days gone by ; to act in thought
Past seasons o'er, and be again a child ;
To sit in fancy on the turf-clad slope
Down which the child would roll ; to pluck gay
      flowers,
Make posies in the sun, which the child's hand
(Childhood offended soon, soon reconciled)
Would throw away, and straight take up again,
Then fling them to the winds, and o'er the lawn
Bound with so playful and so light a foot,
That the pressed daisy scarce declined her head.

*Charles Lamb.*

## THE CHILDREN.

BEAUTIFUL the children's faces!
　　Spite of all that mars and sears;
To my inmost heart appealing;
Calling forth love's tenderest feeling;
　　Steeping all my soul with tears.

Eloquent the children's faces —
　　Poverty's lean look, which saith,
" Save us! save us! woe surrounds us;
Little knowledge sore confounds us;
　　Life is but a lingering death.

" Give us light amid our darkness;
　　Let us know the good from ill;
Hate us not for all our blindness;
Love us, lead us, show us kindness —
　　You can make us what you will.

" We are willing, we are ready;
　　We would learn if you would teach;
We have hearts that yearn to duty;
We have minds alive to beauty;
　　Souls that any heights can reach.

" Raise us by your Christian knowledge ;
　Consecrate to man our powers ;
Let us take our proper station ;
We, the rising generation,
　Let us stamp the age as ours.

" We shall be what you will make us —
　Make us wise and make us good !
Make us strong in time of trial ;
Teach us temperance, self-denial,
　Patience, kindness, fortitude.

" Look into our childish faces ;
　See ye not our willing hearts ?
Only love us — only lead us ;
Only let us know you need us,
　And we all will do our parts.

" We are thousands — many thousands ;
　Every day our ranks increase ;
Let us march beneath your banner,
We, the legion of true honor,
　Combating for love and peace.

" Train us ; try us ; days slide onward,
　They can ne'er be ours again ;
Save us ! save, from our undoing !
Save from ignorance and ruin ;
　Make us worthy to be men !

" Send us to our weeping mothers,
    Angel-stamped in heart and brow ;
We may be our fathers' teachers ;
We may be the mightiest preachers
    In the day that dawneth now ! "

Such the children's mute appealing.
    All my inmost soul was stirred ;
And my heart was bowed with sadness,
When a cry, like summer's gladness,
    Said, " The children's prayer is heard."

                              *Mary Howitt.*

## THE WONDERFU' WEAN.

OUR wean's the most wonderfu' wean I e'er saw !
It would tak me a lang simmer day to tell a'
His pranks, frae the mornin' till night shuts his ee ;
When he sleeps like a peerie, 'tween his father
    and me.
For in his quite turns siccan questions he'll speir :
How the moon can stick up in the sky that's sae
    clear ?
What gars the wind blaw ? and where frae comes
    the rain ?
He's a perfect divert — he's a wonderfu' wean !

Or wha was the first body's father ? and wha
Made the very first snaw-shower that ever did fa' ?
And wha made the first bird that sang on a tree ?
And the water that swims a' the ships in the sea ?
But after I've told him as weel as I ken,
Again he begins with his wha and his when ;
And he looks ay so wistfu' the whiles I explain ;
He's auld as the hills — he's an auld farrard wean.

And faulk wha hae skill o' the bumps on the head,
Hint there's more ways than toilin' o' winnin'
    , ane's bread ;
Gar he'll be a rich man, and hae men to work for
    him,
Wi' a kyte like a ballie's, shug-shuggin' afory him ;

Wi' a face like the moon — sober, sonsy, and douce,
And a back, for its breadth, like the side o' a house.
Tweel! I'm unco ta'en up wi't — they mak a' sae'
      plain,
He's just a town's talk; he's a by-ord'nar wean!

I ne'er can forget sic a laugh as I gat,
To see him put on father's waistcoat and hat;
Then the lang-leggit boots gaed sae far owre his
      knees,
The tap-loops wi' his fingers he grippit wi' eese;
Then he marched through the house, he marched
      but, he marched ben,
Like owre many more o' our great little men,
That I leuch clean outright, for I cou'dna contain,
He was sic a conceit — sic an ancient-like wean!

But 'mid a' his daffin sic kindness he shows,
That he's dear to my heart as the dew to the rose;
And the unclouded hinny-beam ay in his ee,
Makes him every day dearer and dearer to me.
Though Fortune be saucy, and dirty and dour,
And glower through her fingers like hills through
      a door,
When bodies hae got a bit bit bairn o' their ain,
How he cheers up their hearts! — he's a wonderfu'
      wean!

                        *William Miller.*

## THE MOTHER'S GIFT.

ADDRESSED " TO MY CHARLIE," WITH A BIBLE.

So young you cannot pleasure take
In this — but for your mother's sake,
  The gift you will not spurn;
And O, my child, in after years,
When forced to weep life's bitter tears,
  Then to this volume turn.


Too young thou art to prize it now,
With merry laugh and sunny brow,
  But when by earth's cares driven,
You'll love to read of rest above,
And prize it for a mother's love,
  With which, dear boy, 'tis given.


When tempted, love, to go astray,
Pause, pause, my child! O, turn away
  From sin's alluring form;
Go to thy chamber, and when there,
Seek in thy mother's gift, and prayer,
  A refuge from the storm.

Read, my dear son, "believe and live,"
Then not in vain this book I give
　To my own darling boy;
'Twill smooth for thee life's thorny path,
Teach thee to shun thy Maker's wrath,
　And wear his "crown of joy."


When grief shall check thy young heart's
　　mirth,
To weep that she who gave thee birth
　Has passed into the skies;
Then ponder o'er thy mother's gift,
It will thy drooping spirit lift,
　And dry those streaming eyes.


And as your hand its pages turn,
Resolve, dear boy, of Christ to learn,
　Be lowly, meek, and mild;
Remember, she who gave this book,
May, though unseen, upon thee look,
　Rejoicing in her child.


But, if with grief I am appalled,
That thou shouldst be "the early called,"
　And I "the left to weep;"
Then may this book — my gift to thee —
Support my soul, my solace be,
　Till by thy side I sleep.

## THE LITTLE GIRL'S SONG.

Do not mind my crying, papa, — I am not cry-
    ing for pain ;
Do not mind my shaking, papa, — I am not
    shaking with fear ;
Though the wild wind is hideous to hear,
And I see the snow and the rain —
When will you come back again,
Papa, papa?

Somebody else that you love, papa,
Somebody else that you dearly love
Is weary, like me, because you're away.
Sometimes I see her lips tremble and move,
And I seem to know what they are going to say ;
And every day, and all the long day,
I long to cry, " O mamma, mamma!
When will papa come back again? "
But before I can say it I see the pain
Creeping up on her white, white cheek,
As the sweet, sad sunshine creeps up the white
    wall ;
And then I am sorry, and fear to speak :
And slowly the pain goes out of her cheek,
As the sad, sweet sunshine goes from the wall.

O, I wish I were grown up wise and tall!
That I might throw my arms around her neck,
And say, " Dear mamma, O, what is it all
That I see, and see, and do not see,
In your white face all the live-long day ? "
But she hides her grief from a child like me.
When will you come back again,
Papa, papa?

Where were you going, papa, papa ?
All this long while have you been on the sea?
When she looks as if she saw far away,
Is she thinking of you, and what does she see ?
Are the white sails blowing,
And the blue men rowing,
And are you standing on the high deck
Where we saw you stand till the ship grew gray,
And we watched and watched till the ship was a
        speck,
And the dark came first to you, far away ?
I wish I could see what she can see,—
But she hides her grief from a child like me.
When will you come back again,
Papa, papa?

Don't you remember, papa, papa,
How we used to sit by the fire all three,
And she told me tales while I sat on her knee,
And heard the winter winds roar down the street,
And knocked like men at the window pane ?

And the louder they roared, O, it seemed more
    sweet
To be warm and warm as we used to be,
Sitting at night by the fire, all three.
When will you come back again,
Papa, papa?


Papa, I like to sit by the fire;
Why does she sit far away in the cold?
If I had but somebody wise and old,
That every day I might cry and say,
" Is she changed, do you think, or do I forget?
Was she always as white as she is to-day?
Did she never carry her head up higher? "
Papa, papa, if I could but know!
Do you think her voice was always so low?
Did I always see what I seem to see
When I wake up at night and her pillow is wet?
You used to say her hair it was gold —
It looks like silver to me.
But still she tells the same tale that she told,
She sings the same songs when I sit on her knee,
And the house goes on as it went long ago,
When we lived together, all three.
Sometimes my heart seems to sink, papa,
And I feel as if I could be happy no more.
Is she changed, do you think, papa,
Or did I dream she was brighter before?

She makes me remember my snowdrop, papa,
That I forgot in thinking of you,
The sweetest snowdrop that ever I knew!
But I put it out of the sun and the rain;
It was green and white when I put it away,
It had one sweet bell and green leaves four;
It was green and white when I found it that day,
It had one pale bell and green leaves four;
But I was not glad of it any more.
Was it changed, do you think, papa,
Or did I dream it was brighter before?

Do not mind my crying, papa,
I am not crying for pain.
Do not mind my shaking, papa,
I am not shaking for fear,
Though the wild, wild wind is hideous to hear,
And I see the snow and the rain.
When will you come back again,
Papa, papa?

*Sidney Dobell.*

## WE ARE SEVEN.

A SIMPLE child, dear brother Jim,
 That lightly draws its breath,
And feels its life in every limb,
 What should it know of death?

I met a little cottage girl;
 She was eight years old, she said;
Her hair was thick with many a curl
 That clustered round her head.

She had a rustic woodland air,
 And she was wildly clad;
Her eyes were fair, and very fair —
 Her beauty made me glad.

" Sisters and brothers, little maid,
 How many may you be? "
" How many? seven in all," she said,
 And wondering looked at me.

" And where are they? I pray you tell."
 She answered, " Seven are we;
And two of us at Conway dwell,
 And two are gone to sea.

" Two of us in the churchyard lie,
    My sister and my brother;
And in the churchyard-cottage, I
    Dwell near them, with my mother."

" You say that two at Conway dwell,
    And two are gone to sea,
Yet ye are seven! I pray you tell,
    Sweet maid, how this may be?"

Then did the little maid reply,
    " Seven boys and girls are we;
Two of us in the churchyard lie,
    Beneath the churchyard tree."

" You run about, my little maid,
    Your limbs they are alive;
If two are in the churchyard laid,
    Then ye are only five."

' Their graves are green; they may be seen,"
    The little maid replied,
" Twelve steps or more from my mother's door,
    And they are side by side.

" My stockings there I often knit,
    My kerchief there I hem;
And there upon the ground I sit—
    I sit and sing to them.

" And often after sunset, sir,
    When it is light and fair,
I take my little porringer,
    And eat my supper there.

" The first that died was little Jane;
    In bed she moaning lay,
Till God released her of her pain,
    And then she went away.

" So in the churchyard she was laid;
    And all the summer dry,
Together round her grave we played —
    My brother John and I.

"And when the ground was white with snow,
    And I could run and slide,
My brother John was forced to go —
    And he lies by her side."

" How many are you, then," said I,
    " If they two are in heaven?"
The little maiden did reply,
    " O master! we are seven."

" But they are dead; those two are dead!
    Their spirits are in heaven!"
'Twas throwing words away; for still
The little maid would have her will,
    And said, " Nay, we are seven!"

## MY CHILD.

I CANNOT make him dead !
His fair, sunshiny head
Is ever bounding round my study chair ;
Yet, when my eyes, now dim
With tears, I turn to him,
The vision vanishes — he is not there.

I walk my parlor floor,
And through the open door
I hear a footfall on the chamber stair ;
I'm stepping towards the hall
To give the boy a call ;
And then bethink me that he is not there.

I thread the crowded street, —
A satchelled lad I meet,
With the same beaming eyes and colored hair ;
And, as he's running by,
Follow him with my eye,
Scarcely believing that he is not there.

I know his face is hid
Under the coffin lid ;
Closed are his eyes ; cold is his forehead fair :
My hand that marble felt ;
O'er it in prayer I knelt ;
Yet my heart whispers that he is not there.

I cannot make him dead !
When passing by the bed,
So long watched over with parental care,
My spirit and my eye
Seek him inquiringly,
Before the thought comes that he is not there.


When, at the cool, gray break
Of day, from sleep I wake,
With my first breathing of the morning air
My soul goes up, with joy,
To Him who gave my boy ;
Then comes the sad thought that he is not there.


When at the day's calm close,
Before we seek repose,
I'm with his mother, offering up our prayer ;
Whate'er I may be saying,
I am in spirit praying
For our boy's spirit, though he is not there.


Not there !   Where, then, is he ?
The form I used to see
Was but the raiment that he used to wear ;
The grave, that now doth press
Upon that cast-off dress,
Is but his wardrobe locked — he is not there.

He lives!   In all the past
He lives; nor, to the last,
Of seeing him again will I despair :
In dreams I see him now,
And on his angel-brow
I see it written, " Thou shalt see me *there*."

Yes, we all live to God !
Father, thy chastening rod,
So help us, thine afflicted ones, to bear,
That, in the spirit-land,
Meeting at thy right hand,
'Twill be our heaven to find that he is there.

*John Pierpont.*

TO A CHILD.

THY memory, as a spell
    Of love, comes o'er my mind ;
As dew upon the purple bell —
    As perfume on the wind —
As music on the sea —
    As sunshine on the river ; —
So hath it always been to me,
    So shall it be forever.

I hear thy voice in dreams,
  Upon me softly call,
Like echoes of the mountain streams,
  In sportive waterfall.
I see thy form as when
  Thou wert a living thing,
And blossomed in the eyes of men
  Like any flower of spring.

Thy soul to heaven hath fled,
  From earthly thraldom free;
Yet, 'tis not as the dead
  That thou appear'st to me.
In slumber I behold
  Thy form, as when on earth,
Thy locks of waving gold,
  Thy sapphire eye of mirth.

I hear, in solitude,
  The prattle kind and free,
Thou utteredst in joyful mood
  While seated on my knee.
So strong each vision seems,
  My spirit that doth fill,
I think not they are dreams,
  But that thou livest still.

## MY BOY.

IT is his birthday — ask me not
  Why sadness dwells upon my brow;
The past can never be forgot;
  My angel boy is with me now!
Ye see no tear — ye hear no groan —
Nay, all my tears are shed alone!

My heart is full; but still no sigh
  Shall mar the joy that others feel;
I've tried, and ever mean to try,
  To share a part in others' weal.
I love each flower that God hath made,
In garden-walk or greenwood glade.

It is six years this very day,
  Since first I smiled upon my boy;
The gift upon my bosom lay,
  A mother's only pride and joy!
My first-born darling was at rest
Upon her heavenly Father's breast!

One cherished bud was early torn
  From earth, to bloom in Paradise!
For weeks and months I sadly mourned,
  Nor dreamed that God would chasten *twice*!

I thought he sent my angel boy
To bring back love, and health, and joy.

The spoiler's hand was not content ; —
  I loved, and loved, alas, too well !
The treasure from my heart was rent ; —
  Life of my life, farewell ! farewell !
My Father knew a heart like mine
Worshipped too wildly at earth's shrine.

I have a long dark chestnut curl,
  Which seems to form of life a part ;
Not all the riches of this world
  Could tempt the treasure from my heart.
O, what is this earth's glittering gold,
When *love's* dear treasures have been sold ?

Each treasure of the past I shrine ;
  I've garnered up thy books, my boy ;
No child shall touch what once was thine ;
  No rude hand mar one single toy.
O, call me selfish, if ye will,
And strive love's warm wild gush to still.

Ye gaze upon my tearless eye,
  Ye see me smile when others smile ;
But when I to my chamber hie,
  'Tis there I grieve like some lone child !
Tears are too sacred gems to fall,
To attract the gaze of one and all.

Ye say that grief grows less with time ;
　A mother's heart forget to feel !
Go, bid the sun to cease to shine !
　Yon starry heavens their gems to yield !
There's One who reads my inmost soul ;
He knows my love will ne'er grow cold.

*Mrs. R. T. Eldredye.*

---

## THE LITTLE SLEEPER.

SHE sleeps ; but the soft breath
No longer stirs her golden hair, —
The robber hand of Death
Has stolen thither unaware ;
The lovely edifice
Is still as beautiful and fair,
But mournfully we miss
The gentle habitant that sojourned there.

With stealthy pace he crept
To the guest-chamber where it lay —
That angel-thing — and slept,
And whispered it to come away ;
He broke the fairy lute
That, light with laughter, used to play,
And left all dull and mute
The silver strings that tinkled forth so gay.

Then with his finger cold
He shut the glancing windows too;
With fringe of drooping gold
He darkened the small panes of blue;
Sheer from the marble floor
He swept the flowers of crimson hue;
He closed the ivory door,
And o'er the porch the rosy curtains drew.


The angel-guest is gone,
Upon the spoiler's dark wing borne;
The road she journeys on
Wends evermore, without return.
To ruin and decay
The fairy palace now must turn;
For the sun's early ray
Upon its walls and windows shall not play,
Nor light its golden roof to-morrow morn.

## LITTLE JANE.

LITTLE Jane came dancing
Into the sunny room,
" And what do you think, papa? " she cried,
" I saw the father of Ellen who died,
And the men who were making her tomb ;
And the father patted me on the head
All for the sake of her who is dead,
And gave me this doll, and wept, and said
That I was my papa's pride ! "
" And so you are," with an accent wild,
Said the widower wan, — " Come here, my
          child ! "

Ah, but her locks were fair and bright ;
O, but her eyes were full of light,
And her little feet danced in ceaseless play.
" Always be glad, always be gay,
Sing and romp, and never be sad,
So you will make your papa glad."

And the little one bounded from his knee,
Lifted her doll, and screamed with glee,
As the sunlight fell on the floor ;
But who is he at the open door,
Waiting, watching evermore, —

Whose fellow none may see, —
Who came unbidden once before,
And hushed the harp in the corner there,
And filled one heart with the wild despair
Of the endless Nevermore?

Stealthy his touch, and stealthy his tread;
He lays his hand on her sunny head;
And who may mention the grace that has fled,
Or paint the bloom of light that is dead?

The Present rushes into the Past —
Nothing on earth is doomed to last;
Summer is ended, and winter is near,
Rain is steaming on moor and mere,
Dead leaves are on the blast;
The shutters are up in the empty room, —
Nothing to break its hush of gloom,
Nothing but gusts of plashing rain
Beating against the window pane,
Mingled with brine swirled up from the sea,
And thoughts of that which used to be
And cannot be again.

*J. Stanyan Bigg.*

## THE DYING BOY'S REQUEST.

O, TAKE me home, mother,
  Where the brook goes babbling by,
And where the thrush pours forth his song
  O, take me home to die;
I yearn to see my old playground,
  Where I played in childhood's morn,
And I yearn to lay on my little cot
  In the room where I was born.
You'll plant sweet flowers on my grave —
  Say, mother, will you not?
You'll lay me by the mossy bank —
  I've told you of the spot;
'Tis close by the church, dear mother,
  And when you kneel to pray,
I'll listen to your humble words,
  Though I'll be far away.
I feel I'm dying now, kind mother;
  O, take me to your breast,
And let me hear your loving voice
  Ere I shall sink to rest;
O, there's dimness on my sight, mother;
  I cannot get my breath;
Is it your sobs I hear, mother?
  O, tell me, is this death?

*George Boudwin.*

## DIRGE OF A CHILD.

No bitter tears for thee be shed,
  Blossom of being, seen and gone!
With flowers alone we strew thy bed,
  O, blest departed one!
Whose all of life, a rosy ray,
Blessed into dawn, and passed away.

Yes, thou art fled, ere guilt had power
  To stain thy cherub-soul and form;
Closed is the soft, ephemeral flower,
  That never felt a storm, —
The sunbeam's smile, the zephyr's breath,
All that it knew from birth to death.

Thou wert so like a form of light,
  That heaven benignly called thee hence,
Ere yet the world could breathe one blight
  O'er thy sweet innocence;
And thou, that brighter home to bless,
Art passed, with all thy loveliness.

O, hadst thou still on earth remained,
  Vision of beauty, fair as brief!
How soon thy brightness had been stained
  With passion or with grief!

Now, not a sullying breath can rise,
To dim thy glory in the skies.

We rear no marble o'er thy tomb;
  No sculptured image there shall mourn;
Ah, fitter far the vernal bloom
  Such dwelling to adorn.
Fragrance, and flowers, and dews must be
The only emblems meet for thee.

Thy grave shall be a blessèd shrine,
  Adorned with Nature's brightest wreath;
Each glowing season shall combine
  Its incense there to breathe,
And oft, upon the midnight air,
Shall viewless harps be murmuring there.

And, O, sometimes in visions blest,
  Sweet spirit, visit our repose,
And bear from thine own world of rest
  Some balm for human woes!
What form more lovely could be given,
Than thine, to messenger of heaven?

*Mrs. Hemans.*

## THE ANGEL'S STORY.

THROUGH the blue and frosty heavens,
  Christmas stars were shining bright;
The glistening lamps of the great city
  Almost matched their gleaming light;
And the winter snow was lying,
And the winter winds were sighing,
  Long ago, one Christmas night.


While from every tower and steeple,
  Pealing bells were sounding clear,
(Never with such tones of gladness,
  Save when Christmas time is near,)
Many a one that night was merry,
  Who had toiled through all the year.


That night saw old wrongs forgiven,
  Friends, long parted, reconcile;
Voices, all unused to laughter,
  Eyes that had forgot to smile,
Anxious hearts that feared the morrow,
  Freed from all their cares a while.

6

Rich and poor felt the same blessing
  From the gracious season fall;
Joy and plenty in the cottage,
  Peace and feasting in the hall;
And the voices of the children
  Ringing clear above it all!

Yet one house was dim and darkened;
  Gloom, and sickness, and despair,
Abiding in the gilded chamber,
  Climbing up the marble stair,
Stilling e'en the voice of mourning
  For a child lay dying there.

Silken curtains fell around him,
  Velvet carpets hushed the tread,
Many costly toys were lying,
  All unheeded, by his bed;
And his tangled golden ringlets
  Were on downy pillows spread.

All the skill of the great city
  To save that little life was vain;
That little thread from being broken;
That fatal word from being spoken;
  Nay, his very mother's pain,
And the mighty love within her,
  Could not give him health again.

And she knelt there still beside him,
　　She alone with strength to smile,
And to promise he should suffer
　　No more in a little while,
And with murmured song and story,
　　The long, weary hours beguile.


Suddenly an unseen Presence
　　Checked these constant mourning cries,
Stilled the little heart's quick fluttering,
　　Raised the blue and wondering eyes,
Fixed on some mysterious vision,
　　With a startled, sweet surprise ; —


For a radiant angel hovered,
　　Smiling, o'er the little bed ;
White his raiment, from his shoulders
　　Snowy dove-like pinions spread,
And a starlike light was shining,
　　In a glory round his head.


While, with tender love, the angel,
　　Leaning o'er the little nest,
In his arms the sick child folding,
　　Laid him gently on his breast ;
Sobs and wailings from the mother,
　　And her darling was at rest.

So the angel, slowly rising,
  Spread his wings ; and, through the air,
Bore the pretty child, and held him
  On his heart with loving care,
A red branch of blooming roses
  Placing softly by him there.


While the child thus clinging, floated
  Towards the mansions of the blest,
Gazing from his shining guardian
  To the flowers upon his breast,
Thus the angel spake, still smiling
  On the little heavenly guest :


" Know, O little one ! that heaven
  Does no earthly thing disdain.
Man's poor joys find there an echo,
  Just as surely as his pain ;
Love, on earth so feebly striving,
  Lives divine in heaven again ! "

## THE LITTLE FROCK.

A COMMON light-blue muslin frock
   Is hanging on the wall,
But no one in the household now
   Can wear a dress so small.

The sleeves are both turned inside out,
   And tell of summer wear;
They seem to wait the owner's hands
   Which last year hung them there.

'Twas at the children's festival
   Her Sunday dress was soiled —
You need not turn it from the light —
   To me it is not spoiled.

A sad and yet a pleasant thought
   Is to the spirit told,
By this dear little rumpling thing,
   With dust in every fold.

Why should men weep that to their home
   An angel's love is given —
Or that, before them, she is gone
   To blessedness in heaven?

## THE DYING CHILD.

"COME closer, closer, dear mamma,
 My heart is filled with fears ;
My eyes are dark ; I hear your sobs,
 But cannot see your tears.

"I feel your warm breath on my lips
 That are so icy cold ;
Come closer, closer, dear mamma,
 Give me your hand to hold.

"I quite forget my little hymn,
 'How doth the busy bee,'
Which every day I used to say,
 When sitting on your knee.

"Nor can I recollect my prayers ;
 And, dear mamma, you know
That the great God will angry be
 If I forget them too.

"And dear papa, when he comes home,
 O, will not he be vexed?
'Give us this day our daily bread '—
 What is it that comes next?"

"Hush, darling ; you are going to
 The bright and blessèd sky,
Where all God's blessèd children go,
 To live with him on high."

" But will he love me, dear mamma,
      As tenderly as you ?
And will my own papa, one day,
      Come and live with me, too ?

" But you must first lay me to sleep
      Where grandpapa is laid ; —
Is not the churchyard cold and dark ?
      ' And shan't I be afraid ?

" And will you every evening come,
      And say my pretty prayer
Over poor Lucy's little grave,
      And see that no one's there ?

" And promise me that when you die,
      That they your grave shall make
Next unto mine, that I may be
      Close to you when I wake.

" Nay, do not leave me, dear mamma ;
      Your watch beside me keep.
My heart feels cold — the room's all dark ; .
      ' Now lay me down to sleep.'

" And should I sleep to wake no more,
      Dear, dear mamma, good by !
Poor nurse is kind ; but, O, do you
      Be with me when I die ! ' "

## THE LITTLE SLEEPER.

No mother's eye beside thee wakes to-night;
  No taper burns beside thy lonely bed;
Darling, thou liest, hidden out of sight,
  And none are near thee but the silent dead.

How cheerly glows the hearth, yet glows in vain;
  For we, uncheered, beside it sit alone,
And listen to the wild and beating rain,
  In angry gusts against our casement blown.

And though we nothing speak, yet well I know
  That both our hearts are there, where thou dost
    keep
Within thy narrow chamber far below,
  For the first time unwatched, thy lonely sleep.

O, no; not thou! and we our faith deny
  This thought allowing. Thou, removed from
    harms,
In Abraham's bosom dost securely lie;
  O, not in Abraham's, in a Saviour's arms!

In that dear Lord's, who, in thy worst distress.
  Thy bitterest anguish, gave thee, dearest child,
Still to abide in perfect gentleness,
  And, like an angel, to be meek and mild.

Sweet corn of wheat, committed to the ground,
  To die and live, and bear more gracious ear ;
While in the heart of earth thy Saviour found
  His place of rest, for thee we will not fear.

Sleep softly, till that blesséd rain and dew,
  Down lighting upon earth, such change shall
      bring,
That all its fields of death shall laugh anew ;
  Yea, with a living harvest, laugh and sing.

*Dean French.*

---

## ANNIE IN THE GRAVEYARD.

SHE bounded o'er the graves,
  With a buoyant step of mirth ;
She bounded o'er the graves,
Where the weeping willow waves,
  Like a creature not of earth.

Her hair was blown aside,
  And her eyes were glittering bright ;
Her hair was blown aside,
And her little hands spread wide,
  With an innocent delight.

She spelled the lettered word
  That registered the dead ;
She spelled the lettered word,
And her busy thoughts were stirred
  With pleasure as she read.

She stopped and culled a leaf,
  Left fluttering on a rose ;
She stopped and culled a leaf,
Sweet monument of grief,
  That in our churchyard grows.

She culled it with a smile —
  'Twas near her sister's mound ;
She culled it with a smile,
And played with it a while,
  Then scattered it around.

I did not chill her heart,
  Nor turn its gush to tears ;
I did not chill her heart —
O, bitter drops will start
  Full soon in coming years.

*Caroline Gilman.*

## THE ADOPTED CHILD.

" Why wouldst thou leave me, O gentle child ?
Thy home on the mountain is bleak and wild —
A straw-roofed cabin, with lowly wall ;
Mine is a fair and pillared hall,
Where many an image of marble gleams,
And the sunshine of pictures forever streams."

" O, green is the turf where my brothers play,
Through the long bright hours of the summer's
    day ;
They find the red cup-moss where they climb,
And they chase the bee o'er the scented thyme,
And the rocks where the heath-flower blooms
    they know.
Lady, kind lady ! O, let me go."

" Content thee, boy, in my bower to dwell ;
Here are sweet sounds which thou lovest well :
Flutes on the air in the stilly noon,
Harps which the wandering breezes tune,
And the silvery wood-note of many a bird
Whose voice was ne'er in thy mountain heard."

" O, my mother sings at the twilight's fall,
A song of the hills far more sweet than all ;
She sings it under our own green tree,
To the babe half slumbering on her knee.
I dreamed last night of that music low —
Lady, kind lady ! O, let me go."

" Thy mother is gone from her cares to rest ;
She hath taken the babe on her quiet breast ;
Thou wouldst meet her footsteps, my boy, no
    more,
Nor hear her song at the cabin door.
Come thou with me to the vineyards nigh,
And we'll pluck the grapes of the richest dye."

" Is my mother gone from her home away ?
But I know that my brothers are there at play —
I know they are gathering the fox-glove's bell,
Or the long fern leaves by the sparkling well ;
Or they launch their boats where the bright
    streams flow —
Lady, kind lady ! O, let me go."

" Fair child, thy brothers are wanderers now ;
They sport no more on the mountain's brow ;
They have left the fern by the spring's green
    side,
And the streams where the fairy barks were tied.
Be thou at peace in thy brighter lot,
For the cabin home is a lonely spot. '

" Are they gone, all gone, from the sunny hill ?
But the bird and the bluefly rove o'er it still ;
And the red deer bound in their gladness free,
And the heath is bent by the singing bee,
And the waters leap, and the fresh winds blow —
Lady, kind lady ! O, let me go."

*Felicia Hemans.*

## THREE LITTLE GRAVES.

THREE little graves! Talk not of sympathy —
  'Twere vain for human clay
To speak of consolation
  To those weary hearts to-day.
Warmest words that lips could fashion,
  Can but mock the woe
Reigning in that stricken household,
  Where, not long ago,
Echoed happy childish voices
  All the livelong day,
Till an angel came from heaven,
  Bearing them away ; —
Folding one in her white pinions,
  Whispering at the door —
" These are gems *too bright* for earth,
  I must gather more ! "

So she lingered on the threshold,
  O ! so white and chill —
Saying, softly, " One more darling,
  Gentle mother, still."
How she clasps it ! Now she's pleading,
  " Let the little baby come —
We will fold our wings around her,
  Bear her safely home —

We will keep her, O, so pure,
  Spotless, undefiled —
Mother, see your angel band,
  Yet — *another child !* "

Then the white wings softly rustled,
  And the low voice said —
" Mother, let your darlings *sleep*,
  Do not call them *dead.*"

So they made three little graves ;
  Let the sunshine fall,
With its golden haze upon them,
  Bright funereal pall.
Lay the crimson autumn leaves
  On the little graves,
While above, the bending willow
  Sadly, softly waves.

Anguished hearts, bereft and lonely,
  In the angels' keeping
Are your three lost ones to-night —
  No, not dead, but sleeping !

                              *Mrs. B. F. E.*

## TO A CHILD DURING SICKNESS.

SLEEP breathes at last from out thee,
　My little, patient boy ;
And balmy rest about thee
　Smooths off the day's annoy.
I sit me down and think
　Of all thy winning ways ;
Yet almost wish, with sudden shrink,
　That I had less to praise.

Thy sidelong pillowed meekness,
　Thy thanks to all that aid,
Thy heart, in pain and weakness,
　Of fancied faults afraid ;
The little trembling hand
　That wipes thy quiet tears :
These, these are things that may demand
　Dread memories for years.

Sorrows I've had, severe ones,
　I will not think of now,
And calmly, 'midst my dear ones,
　Have wasted with dry brow ;
But when thy fingers press
　And pat my stooping head,
I cannot bear the gentleness —
　The tears are in their bed.

Ah, first-born of thy mother,
    When life and hope were new ;
Kind playmate of thy brother,
    Thy sister, father, too ;
My light, where'er I go ;
    My bird, when prison-bound ;
My hand-in-hand companion — No,
    My prayers shall hold thee round.

To say, " He has departed " —
    " His voice " — " his face " — is gone,
To feel impatient-hearted,
    Yet feel we must bear on —
Ah, I could not endure
    To whisper of such woe,
Unless I felt this sleep insure
    That it will not be so.

Yes, still he's fixed, and sleeping !
    This silence, too, the while —
Its very hush and creeping
    Seem whispering us a smile ;
Something divine and dim
    Seems going by one's ear,
Like parting wings of cherubim,
    Who says, " We've finished here."

                    *Leigh Hunt.*

## SIX LITTLE FEET ON THE FENDER.

IN my heart there liveth a picture
  Of a kitchen rude and old,
Where the firelight tripped o'er the rafters,
  And reddened the roof's brown mould ;
Gilding the steam from the kettle
  That hummed on the foot-worn hearth,
Throughout all the livelong evening
  Its measures of drowsy mirth.

Because of the three light shadows
  That frescoed that rude old room —
Because of the voices echoed
  Up 'mid the rafters' gloom —
Because of the feet on the fender,
  Six restless, white little feet —
The thoughts of that dear old kitchen
  Are to me so fresh and sweet.

When then the first dash on the window
  Told of the coming rain,
O ! where are the fairy young faces
  That crowded against the pane ?
What bits of firelight stealing
  Their dimpled cheeks between,
Went struggling out in the darkness
  In shreds of silver sheen !

Two of the feet grew weary,
　　One dreary, dismal day,
And we tied them with snow-white ribbons,
　　Leaving them there by the way.
There was fresh clay on the fender
　　That weary, wintry night,
For the four little feet had tracked it
　　From his grave on the bright hill's height.

O! why, on this darksome evening,
　　This evening of rain and sleet,
Rest my feet all alone on the hearthstone?
　　O! where are those other feet?
Are they treading the pathway of virtue
　　That will bring us together above?
Or have they made steps that will dampen
　　A sister's tireless love?

## THE LITTLE BOY THAT DIED.

Dr. Chalmers is said to be the author of the following beautiful poem, written on the occasion of the death of a young son whom he greatly loved.

I AM all alone in my chamber now,
  And the midnight hour is near,
And the fagot's crack and the clock's dull tick,
  Are the only sounds I hear;
And over my soul, in its solitude,
  Sweet feelings of sadness glide,
For my heart and my eyes are full when I think
  Of the little boy that died.


I went one night to my father's house —
  Went home to the dear ones all —
And softly I opened the garden gate,
  And softly the door of the hall.
My mother came out to meet her son —
  She kissed me, and then she sighed,
And her head fell on my neck, and she wept
  For the little boy that died.

I shall miss him when the flowers come,
 In the garden where he played;
I shall miss him more by the fireside,
 When the flowers have all decayed;
I shall see his toys and his empty chair,
 And his horse he used to ride,
And they will speak with a silent speech,
 Of the little boy that died.


We shall go home to our Father's house —
 To our Father's house in the skies,
Where the hope of our souls shall have no bl
 Our love no broken ties.
We shall roam on the banks of the River of P
 And bathe in its blissful tide,
And one of the joys of our heaven shall be
 The little boy that died.

## DEATH OF THE FIRST-BORN.

YOUNG mother, he is gone!
His dimpled cheek no more will touch thy breast;
    No more the music-tone
Float from his lips, to thine all fondly pressed;
His smile and happy laugh are lost to thee;
Earth must his mother and his pillow be.


    His was the morning hour;
And he had passed in beauty from the day
    A bud, not yet a flower,
Torn, in its sweetness, from the parent spray;
The death-wind swept him to his soft repose,
As frost, in spring-time, blights the early rose.


    Never on earth again
Will his rich accents charm thy listening ear,
    Like some Æolian strain
Breathing at eventide serene and clear;
His voice is choked in dust, and on his eyes
The unbroken seal of peace and silence lies.

And from thy yearning heart,
Whose inmost core was warm with love for him
    A gladness must depart,
And those kind eyes with many tears be dim;
While lonely memories, an unceasing train,
Will turn the raptures of the past to pain.


    Yet, mourner, while the day
Rolls like the darkness of a funeral by,
    And Hope forbids one ray
To stream across the grief-discolored sky,
There breaks upon thy sorrow's evening gloom
A trembling lustre from beyond the tomb.


    'Tis from the better land!
There, bathed in radiance that around them
        springs,
    Thy loved one's wings expand;
As with the choiring cherubim he sings,
And all the glory of that God can see,
Who said, on earth, to children, "Come to me."


    Mother, thy child is blessed;
And though his presence may be lost to thee,
    And vacant leave thy breast,
And missed, a sweet load from thy parent knee;
Though tones familiar from thine ear have passed
Thou'lt meet thy first-born with his Lord at last.

                    *Willis Gaylord Clark.*

## A PRAYER IN SICKNESS.

SEND down thy wingéd angel, God,
    Amid this night so wild,
And bid him come where now we watch,
    And breathe upon our child.

She lies upon her pillow, pale,
    And moans within her sleep,
Or wakeneth with a patient smile,
    And striveth not to weep.

How gentle and how good a child
    She is, we know too well ;
And dearer to her parents' hearts
    Than our weak words can tell.

We love — we watch throughout the night,
    To aid when need may be ;
We hope — and have despaired at times :
    But now we turn to Thee !

Send down thy sweet-souled angel, God,
    Amid the darkness wild,
And bid him soothe our souls to-night,
    And heal our gentle child !

*Proctor.*

## THE YOUNG GRAY HEAD.

" I'm thinking that to-night, if not before,
There'll be wild work.   Dost hear old Chewtoi
    roar ?
It's brewing up down westward ; and look there
One of those sea-gulls ! — ay, there goes a pair
And such a sudden thaw !  If rain comes on,
As threats, the waters will be out anon.
That path by the ford's a nasty bit of way —  ·
Best let the young ones bide from school to-day.'

The children themselves join in this request
but the mother resolves that they should set ou'
— the two girls, Lizzy and Jenny, the one fivι
and the other seven.  As the dame's will wai
law, so,

                One last fond kiss —
" God bless my little maids ! " the father said ;
And cheerily went his way to win their bread.

Prepared for their journey, they depart witl
the mother's admonitions to the elder, —
            " Now, mind and bring
Jenny safe home," the mother said.  " Don'
    stay
To pull a bough or berry by the way ;

And when you come to cross the ford, hold fast
Your little sister's hand till you're quite past —
That plank's so crazy, and so slippery,
If not o'erflowed, the stepping stones will be.
But you're good children — steady as old folk ;
I'd trust ye any where." Then Lizzy's cloak
(A good gray duffle) lovingly she tied,
And ample little Jenny's lack supplied
With her own warmest shawl. " Be sure," said
 she,
" To wrap it round, and knot it carefully
(Like this) when you come home — just leaving
 free
One hand to hold by. Now, make haste away —
Good will to school, and then good right to
 play."


The mother watched them as they went down
the lane, overburdened with something like a foreboding of evil which she strove to overcome ; but
could not during the day quite bear up against
her own thoughts, more especially as the threat-
ened storm did at length truly set in. His labor
done, the husband makes his three miles way
homeward, until his cottage coming into view, all
its pleasant associations of spring, summer, and
autumn, with its thousand family delights, rush
on his heart :

There was a treasure hidden in his hat —
A plaything for his young ones.  He had foun
A dormouse nest ; the living ball coiled round
For its long winter sleep ; and all his thought,
As he trudged stoutly homeward, was of nough
But the glad wonderment in Jenny's eyes,
And graver Lizzy's quieter surprise,
When he should yield, by guess, and kiss, an
  prayer,
Hard won, the frozen captive to their care.

Out rushes his fondling dog Tinker, but no lit
tle faces greet him as wont at the threshold ; an
to his hurried question, " Are they come ? " —
'twas " No."

To throw his tools down, hastily unhook
The old cracked lantern from its dusty nook,
And while he lit it, speak a cheering word
That almost choked him, and was scarcel
  heard,
Was but a moment's act ; and he was gone
To where a fearful foresight led him on.

A neighbor accompanies him, and they strik
into the track which the children should hav
taken in their way back — now calling aloud o
them through the pitchy darkness, and now, b
the lantern-light, scrutinizing " thicket, hole, an

nook," till the dog, brushing past them with a
bark, shows them that he was on their track:

"Hold the light
Low down — he's making for the water. Hark!
I know that whine — the old dog's found them,
    Mark."
So speaking, breathlessly he hurried on
Toward the old crazy foot-bridge. It was gone!
And all his dull contracted light could show
Was the black void, and dark swollen stream
    below.
"Yet there's life somewhere — more than Tin-
    ker's whine "—
"That's sure," said Mark. "So, let the lantern
    shine
Down yonder. There's the dog — and hark!"
    "O dear!"
And a low sob came faintly on the ear,
Mocked by the sobbing gust. Down, quick as
    thought,
Into the stream leaped Ambrose, where he
    caught
Fast hold of something — a dark huddled heap —
Half in the water, where 'twas scarce knee deep
For a tall man; and half above it, propped
By some old ragged side-piles that had stopped
Endways the broken plank when it gave way
With the two little ones that luckless day!

" My babes! my lambkins!" was the father's
    cry —
*One little voice* made answer, " Here am I ! "
'Twas Lizzy's.  There she crouched, with face
    as white,
More ghastly, by the flickering lantern-light,
Than sheeted corpse.  The pale, blue lips drawn
    tight,
Wide parted, showing all the pearly teeth,
And eyes on some dark object underneath,
Washed by the turbid water, fixed like stone —
One arm and hand stretched out, and rigid
    grown,
Grasping, as in the death-gripe, Jenny's frock.
There she lay drowned.  .   .   .   .
    They lifted her from out her watery bed —
Its covering gone, the lovely little head
Hung like a broken snow-drop, all aside,
And one small hand.  The mother's shawl was
    tied,
Leaving *that* free about the child's small form,
As was her last injunction — " fast and warm ; "
Too well obeyed — too fast !  A fatal hold,
Affording to the scrag, by a thick fold
That caught and pinned her to the river's bed :
While through the reckless water overhead
Her life-breath bubbled up.

I pass over the cruel self-upbraidings of her
mother for —

> " She might have lived,
> Struggling like Lizzie," was the thought that
>     rived
> The wretched mother's heart, when she knew
>     all,
> " But for my foolishness about that shawl " —

a torture aggravated by the tones of the surviving
child, who half deliriously kept on ejaculating —

> " Who says I forgot ?
> Mother ! indeed, indeed I kept fast hold ;
> And tied the shawl quite close — she can't be
>     cold —
> But she won't move — we slept — I don't know
>     how —
> But I held on — and I'm so weary now —
> And it's so dark and cold ! — O dear ! O dear ! —
> And she won't move — if daddy was but here ! "

From their despair for the lost, the poor parents turned to their almost forlorn hope in the
living, as —

> All night long from side to side she turned,
> Piteously plaining like a wounded dove,
> With now and then the murmur, " She won't
>     move."

And, lo ! when morning, as in mockery, bright
Shone on that pillow — passing strange the
    sight —
The young head's raven hair was streaked with
    white !

Caroline Anne Souther.

---

## TO A CHILD

### EMBRACING HIS MOTHER.

LOVE thy mother, little one !
  Kiss and clasp her neck again, —
Hereafter she may have a son
  Will kiss and clasp her neck in vain.
    Love thy mother, little one !

Gaze upon her living eyes,
  And mirror back her love for thee, —
Hereafter thou mayst shudder sighs
  To meet them when they cannot see.
    Gaze upon her living eyes !

Press her lips the while they glow
  With love that they have often told, —
Hereafter thou mayst press in woe,
  And kiss them till thine own are cold.
    Press her lips the while they glow!

O, revere her raven hair!
  Although it be not silver-gray, —
Too early Death, led on by Care,
  May snatch save one dear lock away.
    O, revere her raven hair!

Pray for her at eve and morn,
  That Heaven may long the stroke defer, —
For thou mayst live the hour forlorn
  When thou wilt ask to die with her.
    Pray for her at eve and morn!

              *Thomas Hood.*

## OVER THE WAY.

GONE in her childish purity
Out from her golden day ;
Fading away in the light so sweet,
Where the silver stars and the sunbeams meet,
Paving a path for her silent feet,
    Over the silent way.

Over her bosom tenderly
The pearl-white hands are pressed ;
The lashes lie on her cheeks so thin —
Where the softest blush of the rose hath been —
Shutting the blue of her eyes within
    The pure lids closed in rest.

Over the sweet brow lovingly
Twineth her sunny hair ;
She was so fragile that Love sent down
From his heavenly gems that soft bright crown,
To shade her brow with its waves so brown,
    Light as the dimpling air.

Gone to sleep with the tender smile
Froze on her silent lips
By the farewell kiss of her dewy breath,
Cold in the clasp of her angel Death —
Like the last fair bud of a fading wreath,
    Whose bloom the white frost nips.

Robin — hushed in your downy bed
Over the swinging bough —
Do you miss her voice from your glad duet,
When the dew in the heart of the rose is set,
Till its velvet lips with the essence wet
        In orient crimson glow?


Rosebud under your shady leaf—
Hid from the sunny day —
Do you miss the glance of the eye so bright,
Whose blue was heaven in your timid sight?
It is beaming now in the world of light,
        Over the starry way.


Hearts — where the darling's head hath lain,
Held by love's shining ray —
Do you know that the touch of her gentle hand
Doth brighten the harp in the unknown land?
O, she waits for us with the angel band
        Over the starry way.

*E. Conwell Smith.*

8

## THE ORPHAN BOY'S TALE.

STAY, lady, stay, for mercy's sake,
 And hear a helpless orphan's tale!
Ah! sure my looks must pity wake,
 'Tis Want that makes my cheek so pale.
Yet I was once a mother's pride,
 And my brave father's hope and joy;
But in the Nile's proud fight he died,
 And I am now an orphan boy.

Poor, foolish child! how pleased was I
 When news of Nelson's victory came,
Along the crowded streets to fly,
 And see the lighted windows flame!
To force me home my mother sought;
 She could not bear to see my joy,
For with my father's life 'twas bought,
 And made me a poor orphan boy.

The people's shouts were long and loud;
 My mother, shuddering, closed her ears;
" Rejoice! rejoice! " still cried the crowd;
 My mother answered with her tears.
" Why are you crying thus," said I,
 " While others laugh and shout with joy? "
She kissed me — and with such a sigh!
 She called me her poor orphan boy.

"What is an orphan boy?" I cried,
  As in her face I looked, and smiled;
My mother through her tears replied,
  "You'll know too soon, ill-fated child!"
And now they've tolled my mother's knell,
  And I'm no more a parent's joy;
O, lady, I have learned too well
  What 'tis to be an orphan boy!


O, were I by your bounty fed!
  Nay, gentle lady, do not chide —
Trust me, I mean to earn my bread;
  The sailor's orphan boy has pride.
Lady, you weep! ha! this to me!
  You'll give me clothing, food, employ?
Look down, dear parents! look, and see
  Your happy, happy orphan boy!

*Amelia Opie.*

## A JUVENILE ACTOR.

Ben Jonson has some pleasing lines on a precocious
in his time, who seems to have been a wonderful acto
" old men " characters.　He died in his thirteenth year,
the poet thus eulogizes him : —

> WEEP with me, all you that read
>     This little story ;
> And know for whom a tear you shed
>     Death's self is sorry.
>
> 'Twas a child that did so thrive
>     In grace and feature,
> That heaven and nature seemed to strive
>     Which owned the creature.
>
> Years he numbered scarce thirteen,
>     When fates turned cruel ;
> Yet three filled zodiacs had he been
>     The stage's jewel.
>
> And did act, what now we moan,
>     Old men so duly,
> As sooth the Parcæ thought him one,
>     He played so truly.

## TO A CHILD BLOWING BUBBLES.

THRICE happy elf! what radiant dreams are thine,
  As thus thou bidd'st thine air-born bubbles
    soar; —
Who would not Wisdom's choicest gifts resign
  To be, like thee, a careless child once more; —

To share thy simple sports and sinless glee;
  Thy breathless wonder, thy unfeigned delight,
As, one by one, those sun-touched glories flee,
  In swift succession, from thy straining sight; —

To feel a power within himself to make,
  Like thee, a rainbow wheresoe'er he goes;
To dream of sunshine, and like thee, to wake
  To brighter visions from his charmed repose; —

Who would not give his all of worldly lore,
  The hard-earned fruits of many a toil and care,
Might he but thus the faded past restore,
  Thy guileless thoughts and blissful ignorance
    share?

Yet life hath bubbles, too, that soothe a while
  The sterner dreams of man's maturer years:

Love, Friendship, Fortune, Fame, by turns be-
    guile,
But melt, 'neath Truth's Ithuriel touch, to tears.

Thrice happy child, a brighter lot is thine!
    What new illusion e'er can match the first?
*We* mourn to see each cherished hope decline;
    *Thy* mirth is loudest when thy bubbles burst.

                         *Alaric Watts.*

## THE BLIND CHILD.

WHERE'S the blind child so admirably fair,
With guileless dimples, and with flaxen hair
That waves in every breeze?   He's often seen
Beyond yon cottage wall, or on the green
With others, matched in spirit and in size —
Health in their cheeks and rapture in their eyes.
That full expanse of voice, to children dear,
Soul of their sports, is duly cherished here.
And hark! that laugh is his — that jovial cry —
He hears the ball and trundling hoop brush by,
And runs the giddy course with all his might —
A very child in every thing but sight —

With circumscribed, but not abated powers,
Play the great object of his infant hours.
In many a game he takes a noisy part,
And shows the native gladness of his heart;
But soon he hears, on pleasure all intent,
The new suggestion, and the quick assent;
The grove invites; delight thrills every breast
To leap the ditch, and seek the downy nest.
Away they start, leave balls and hoops behind,
And *one* companion leave — the boy is *blind!*
His fancy paints their distant paths so gay,
That childish fortitude a while gives way;
He feels his dreadful loss — yet short the pain —
Soon he resumes his cheerfulness again.
Pondering how best his moments to employ,
He sings his little songs of nameless joy,
Creeps on the warm green turf for many an hour,
And plucks, by chance, the white and yellow
    flower;
Smoothing their stems, while resting on his knees,
He binds a nosegay which he never sees;
Along the homeward path then feels his way.

*Bloomfield.*

## THE LITTLE PILGRIM.

I SAW a little pilgrim come
  A sudden to that river,
At whose dark brink bold lips grow dumb,
  And stout hearts quail and quiver,—
  The marge of Death's cold river.

Down to the stream the little maid
  Was led by white-robed angels ;
Around her golden harps they played,
  And sung those sweet evangels
  Sung only by the angels.

Five days upon the brink she lay
  Of that appalling river;
And Death shot arrows every day
  From his insatiate quiver,
  At her, beside the river.

O ! but I stood amazed to hear
  Her wan lips sweetly saying,
" Don't pray to keep me, mamma, dear,
  I must not here be staying."
  Such words of wonder saying !

" Mamma, I do not fear to die,
  My sins are all forgiven ;
And shining angels hovering nigh,
  Will bear my soul to heaven —
  By Jesus quite forgiven."


And then from her fond mother's breast
  She plunged into that river ;
Her fluttering pulses sunk to rest,
  Her heart was still forever,
  And her soul beyond the river.


Now, when my children wait to hear
  Some tender, touching story,
I tell them how, without a fear,
  She died, and went to glory —
  And tears flow with the story.

*Rev. C. W. Richards.*

## CASA WAPPY.

Casa Wappy was the self-conferred pet name of an infant son of the poet, snatched away after a very brief illness.

AND hast thou sought thy heavenly home,
    Our fond, dear boy —
The realms where sorrow dare not come,
    Where life is joy?
Pure at thy death as at thy birth,
Thy spirit caught no taint from earth;
Even by its bliss we mete our dearth,
        Casa Wappy!

Despair was in our last farewell,
    As closed thine eye;
Tears of our anguish may not tell
    When thou didst die;
Words may not paint our grief for thee;
Sighs are but bubbles on the sea
Of our unfathomed agony,
        Casa Wappy!

Thou wert a vision of delight,
    To bless us given;
Beauty embodied to our sight;
    A type of heaven!

So dear to us thou wert, thou art
Even less thine own self than a part
Of mine and of thy mother's heart,
   Casa Wappy!


Thy bright brief day knew no decline —
 'Twas cloudless joy;
Sunrise and night alone were thine,
 Belovéd boy!
This morn beheld thee blithe and gay,
That found thee prostrate in decay,
And ere a third shone clay was clay,
   Casa Wappy!


Gem of our hearth, our household pride,
 Earth's undefiled;
Could love have saved, thou hadst not died,
 Our dear, sweet child!
Humbly we bow to Fate's decree:
Yet had we hoped that Time should see
Thee mourn for us, not us for thee,
   Casa Wappy!


Do what I may, go where I will,
 Thou meet'st my sight;
There dost thou glide before me still,
 A form of light!

I feel thy breath upon my cheek —
I see thee smile, I hear thee speak —
Till, O ! my heart is like to break,
                    Casa Wappy !


Methinks thou smilest before me now,
        With glance of stealth ;
The hair thrown back from thy full brow,
        In buoyant health ;
I see thine eyes' deep violet light,
Thy dimpled cheek carnationed bright,
Thy clasping arms so round and white,
                    Casa Wappy !


The nursery shows thy pictured wall,
        Thy bat, thy bow,
Thy cloak and bonnet, club and ball ;
        But where art thou ?
A corner holds thy empty chair,
Thy playthings idly scattered there,
But speak to us of our despair,
                    Casa Wappy !


Even to the last, thy very word —
        To glad, to grieve —
Was sweet as sweetest song of bird,
        On summer's eve ;

In outward beauty undecayed,
Death o'er thy spirit cast no shade,
And like the rainbow thou didst fade,
   Casa Wappy !


We mourn for thee when blind, blank night
 The chamber fills ;
We pine for thee when morn's first light
 Reddens the hills ;
The sun, the moon, the stars, the sea,
All, to the wall-flower and wild pea,
Are changed — we saw the world through
  thee,
   Casa Wappy !


And though, perchance, a smile may gleam,
 Of casual mirth,
It doth not own, whate'er may seem,
 An inward birth ;
We miss thy small step on the stair ;
We miss thee at our evening prayer ;
All day we miss thee, every where,
   Casa Wappy !


Snows muffled earth when thou didst go,
 In life's spring bloom,
Down to the appointed house below —
 The silent tomb ;

But now the green leaves of the tree,
'The cuckoo, and " the busy bee,"
Return — but with them bring not thee,
   Casa Wappy !

Yet, 'tis sweet balm to our despair,
  Fond, fairest boy,
That heaven is God's, and thou art there
  With him in joy :
There, past are Death, and all its woes ;
There Beauty's stream forever flows,
And Pleasure's day no sunset knows,
   Casa Wappy !

Farewell, then, — for a while, farewell, —
  Pride of my heart !
It cannot be that long we dwell
  Thus torn apart :
Time's shadows like the shuttle flee ;
And, dark howe'er life's night may be,
Beyond the grave I'll meet with thee,
   Casa Wappy !

      *D. M. Moir.*

# INDEX OF FIRST LINES.

———◆———

## (FOR DAYS OF GLADNESS.)

www.ingramcontent.com/pod-product-compliance
Lightning Source LLC
Chambersburg PA
CBHW020407030726
47496CB00007B/2351